FOX'S DREAM

by Tejima

SCHOLASTIC INC.

New York Toronto London Auckland Sydney

In a faraway forest, near a faraway mountain,
it is a cold silent night.

The bears and the chipmunks are asleep for the winter.

Snow covered trees glisten in the moonlight.
Their shadows stretch across the frozen snow.

It is still…

...except for the faint sound of an animal's footsteps.

A fox
walks alone
in the moonlight.

He is cold and hungry, and as he wanders
he searches among the trees.

Suddenly he finds a trail of footprints in the snow.

And in the distance
he sees a flash
of white.

Silent as his shadow,

the fox races through the night.

A snow hare soars
across the frosty hill
and disappears.

Once again the fox is alone,

but he is in a place he has never seen before.

All around him is a forest of ice.
The frozen trees glitter in the moonlight.

Animals of ice nestle in their branches.

And in a tree near
the very end
of the forest,
the fox sees
a family of ice foxes.

He closes his eyes and remembers a spring when the wind was warm and the earth smelled of new grass and wildflowers.

He remembers his family and the nearness of his mother.

He remembers leaping
with his brother and sister
in the warmth of a gentle sun.

But when the fox opens his eyes, the forest is still
covered with snow, the fox family is still made of ice,

and the fox is still alone.

With one last look at the trees,

the fox walks on.

Little by little, the winter sky grows brighter.
The fox sees something standing in a snowy field.

It's a fox. A vixen.
Her fur shines in the morning light.

In a faraway forest, near a faraway mountain,
it is a cold silent morning. The forest is still
except for two foxes who nuzzle in the sunshine.

Soon it will be spring.

ISBN 0-590-45104-9

Text and illustrations copyright © 1985 by Keizaburō Tejima.
American text copyright © 1987 by Philomel Books.
All rights reserved. Published by Scholastic Inc., 730 Broadway, New York, NY 10003, by arrangement with Philomel Books, a division of The Putnam Berkeley Group Inc.

12 11 10 9 8 7 6 5 4 3 2 1   2 3 4 5 6 7/9

Printed in the U.S.A.   08

First Scholastic printing, January 1992